Tom Tirabosco

At the
Same Time

Kane/Miller
BOOK PUBLISHERS

Somewhere in
the world,
a child opens a **book**.

At the same time,
somewhere else...

a fish eats
another fish...

a little girl is

late for school...

a hedgehog

crosses the road...

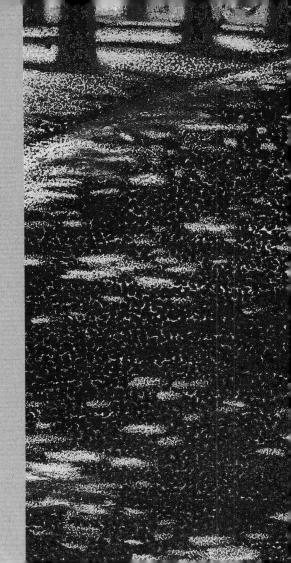

a fox
runs away...

chewing gum
sticks to the
sole of a shoe...

an old man

is bored...

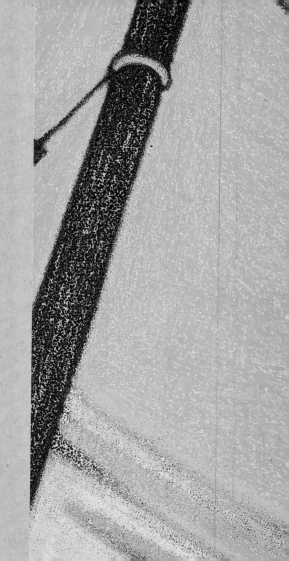

a swallow

flies away...

a fly lands
on a window...

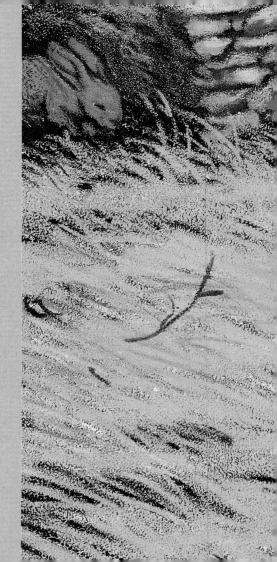

a rabbit
takes shelter
from the wind...

a big
whale dies...

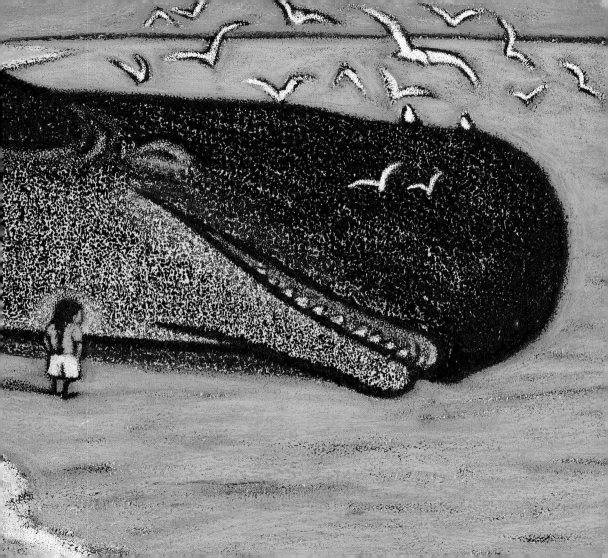

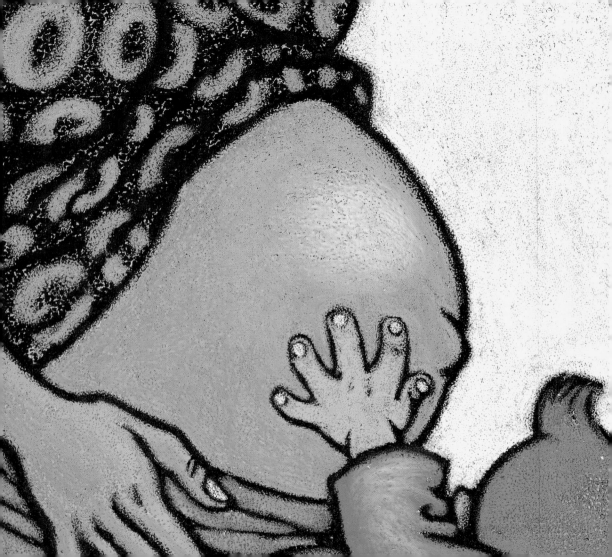

a tummy

moves...

a storm

bursts...

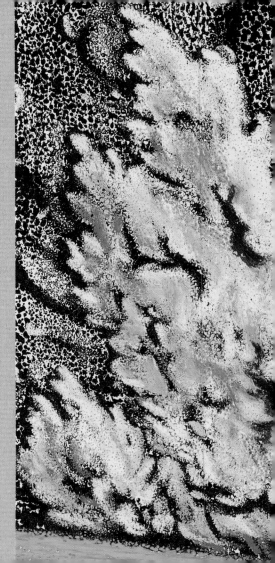

a ball
gets stuck
in a tree...

a cloud
suddenly
changes color...

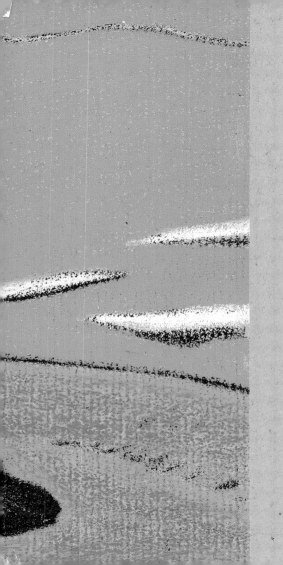

somewhere in
the world,
a child closes
a book.